JENNIFER ARMSTRONG

The Whittler's Tale

PICTURES BY VALERY VASILIEV

TAMBOURINE BOOKS   NEW YORK

To my darlin' Clementine
J.M.A.

To my elder brother, who is my first teacher
V.V.V.

All rights reserved. No part of this book may be reproduced or utilized in any form or by any means, electronic or mechanical, including photocopying, recording, or by any information storage or retrieval system, without permission in writing from the Publisher. Inquiries should be addressed to Tambourine Books, a division of William Morrow & Company, Inc., 1350 Avenue of the Americas, New York, New York 10019. Printed in Singapore. The text type is Monotype Bembo.
Library of Congress Cataloging in Publication Data   Armstrong, Jennifer, 1961–   The whittler's tale/by Jennifer Armstrong; illustrated by Valery Vasiliev.
1st ed. p. cm. Summary: A young girl learns the secret of a strange whittler whose carvings magically come to life. [1. Wood carving—Fiction. 2. Magic—Fiction.]
I. Vasiliev, Valery, ill. II. Title. PZ7.A73367Wh 1994 [E] —dc20 93 -14749 CIP AC ISBN 0-688-10751-6. —ISBN 0-688-10752-4 (lib. bdg.)
1 3 5 7 9 10 8 6 4 2
First edition

One day, Clementine and her friends were playing by the river. The others threw sticks into the water and raced leaf boats in the current. But Clementine sat by herself, humming a tune under her breath and carving a piece of bark with her pocket knife.

When the sun was high, a stranger came along. Clementine watched him from behind a buttercup.

He walked on by, and the children stopped splashing one another to watch. He gave them a friendly smile as he passed, and then he walked beside the riverbank through town. They all followed right behind. Finding a seat in the sunshine, the stranger pulled a small piece of

wood from one pocket and then took a thin, sharp knife from another.
He scratched his head, tapped his chin with one finger, and then began
to carve. Chips and slivers of wood peeled away under his hand, and a
round little bird began to take shape beneath the flashing knife.

"This is the sparrow that flew around the world," the man said. The children crowded in closer, watching. "He has seen the ice-locked mountains of the north, and the broad, brown plains of the south. In the east he saw magical animals formed of water and light, and in the

west he flew past soaring towers and long, arching bridges. Everywhere he went, the sparrow saw strange and wonderful things." Clementine moved closer until she was right by the man's elbow.

His knees were sprinkled with shavings and curls of wood, and his fingers worked steadily around the tiny form. There was a rustling as the sparrow eased his wings and shook the pale dust from his feathers. Clementine let out a sigh.

"And every year, the sparrow took flight again to see the beauty

and wonder of the world," the man finished. He gave the children a smile, and then opened his hands to let the sparrow take wing.

"Ah," they gasped.

Clementine watched in silence as the sparrow winged toward the sky. She touched the man's shoulder. "Please make another," she whispered.

"Yes, another," the other children begged. One by one, grown-ups stopped to watch. The stranger nodded and found several pieces of wood no bigger than eggs. The river chuckled along beside the crowd while

he pared away the first thin slivers and began to speak. He told of the heavenly carp of the sun and moon. He told of the army of valiant mice. He told of the dragonfly that lived inside a volcano.

And all the while, he whittled and carved, and tiny creatures went on
their way, shaking the last wood chips off their scales and feet and wings.
The mayor and his friends watched closely from the edge of the crowd,

and ducked suspiciously as the magical dragonfly sped over their heads.
The townspeople began talking to one another in high, nervous voices.

The mayor cleared his throat. "I'd like to buy that knife from you," he said. But the man shook his head.

"No, I'm sorry. This is a gift from my father. I can't sell it."

The mayor let out his breath in a long, angry hiss. "Everyone go about your business," he shouted. Then he beckoned to his friends and went into the nearby inn to talk.

Clementine moved to the window to listen to the mayor. She knew he was up to no good. "We must get that knife," the mayor was saying. "Don't you see? We can make pieces of gold and precious gems! You saw how the magic knife makes his carvings real."

"Leave this to me," said the sheriff.

The mayor and his friends hurried outside, and the sheriff planted himself in front of the carver. "You have broken several important laws," he announced. "You are practicing a trade without a permit. You are carrying a weapon without a license. And last but not least, you are making a mess!"

"I'm sorry. I didn't know," said the stranger.

"As a fine, hand over that knife and get out of town!"

The stranger threw back his shoulders. "It will do you no good," he warned them solemnly.

"Ha!" the sheriff scoffed. "It will do *you* no good to defy us. Hand over the knife and be quick about it."

The man hung his head. But at last, he slowly raised his hand and let the knife plummet to the ground, where it stuck, point first, and quivered in the silence. Then he turned and walked away.

The mayor and his council retired to the inn to begin carving out their fortunes, and Clementine peeked through the window again.

"Bring me some wood," said the mayor with a cackle.

He grabbed the biggest piece and started to carve. "First I will make a diamond the size of an apple!"

But no matter how he tried, he could not carve an apple-sized diamond or a diamond-sized apple. Twice he jabbed his fingers, and once he nicked his thumb. "This wood is all wrong," he growled.

Finally he threw the wood into the fire and picked up another piece. "This time I will make a gold coin."

But the mayor could not make the knife do what he wanted. Mad
with frustration, he threw the wood and the knife into the fire.

"It was only a trick after all," he decided.

The mayor and his friends felt angry and cheated. With a chorus of

grumbles, they went home. Quietly, cautiously, Clementine slipped into the inn and grabbed a pair of tongs. She pulled the knife from the fire as fast as she could. But the handle was burned through. It crumbled into dust on the hearth.

When the blade was cool enough to touch, she picked it up and ran in search of the whittler. She found him sitting by the river, tossing pebbles into the water. "Excuse me," she said, holding out the blackened blade. "I tried to save your father's gift, but it's ruined. You won't be able to make any more carvings."

He looked at the knife. Then he smiled at Clementine.

"I have another knife," he said. "And I still have my father's gift."

Clementine stared at him. "I don't understand."

"The magic isn't in the knife," the man explained with a wink. "Any old blade will do just fine." He stood up to go. But before he walked away he added, "Try it yourself and see."

For a long time, Clementine stood puzzling over his words. Finally she took out her little pocket knife. Then she found a piece of wood, and sat by herself to think.

The other children were playing their old games again, racing leaf boats and skipping rocks. But Clementine tried very hard and very carefully to carve a bird.

Every moment as she worked, she hoped the bird would take flight. She held her breath and offered the bird to the sky. But although it was perfect, it was only made of wood.

With a sigh, Clementine clasped the bird in her hand and closed her eyes. If only the bird she had carved could be the sparrow that flew

around the world! She imagined it flying over low, grassy slopes dotted
with flowers, and stopping by a clear pool of water.

"On and on the sparrow flew as night fell, and she grew tired searching for a place to rest." Clementine's voice was the merest whisper.

"The wandering bird perched on the walls of a palace, and watched the king's beautiful children play in the garden before she rose up into the sky to continue her journey. For days and nights she flew past cara-

vans crossing the desert, and over the heads of roaming cattle and ante-
lope. The oceans heaved and swelled below her and tossed their foamy
whitecaps up into the night. A year after she started, she smelled the
familiar air of her own country again, and sang with happiness to be
home at last."

In Clementine's hand, the warm, round bird tilted its head and looked up at her. Clementine opened her hands in surprise, and the sparrow hopped onto one finger.

She felt its claws cling to her before it let out one clear, chiming note and took flight. Clementine watched the sparrow dip and soar and flit through the trees.

"Make another one, Clementine."

She looked up, startled, to see the other children watching her. Then Clementine picked up another piece of wood and, with a smile, she began to whittle.